THE PUPPY PLACE

STELLA

THE PUPPY PLACE

Don't miss any of these other stories by Ellen Miles!

STELLA

ELLEN MILES

SCHOLASTIC INC.

ISBN 978-0-545-72643-6

Cover art by Tim O'Brien
Original cover design by Steve Scott

12 11 10 9   17 18 19 20/0

Printed in the U.S.A.   40

First printing, February 2015

CHAPTER ONE

"We should be just about there," said Charles's dad. He peered through the windshield of the van. "Keep an eye out for a sign that says something about Crystal Lake."

"I see it! I see it!"

Charles turned to stare at his younger brother, the Bean. "What are you talking about?" he asked. "You can't read."

The Bean bounced up and down in his car seat. "Can too, can too!" He pointed out the window. "L is for 'lake'!"

Charles swiveled around and stared out his

1

side window just in time to see a large sign that said WELCOME TO CRYSTAL LAKE! Under the words was a picture of a bright blue lake surrounded by pine trees.

"He's right!" Dad put on his blinker. "This must be the road we take."

Charles slumped in his seat, feeling tired even though he'd been sitting still for hours. "I still wish Lizzie was with us," he said. "Or that we could have stayed home with her and that new puppy." This camping trip was supposed to have included all the Peterson kids, but at the last minute his older sister had gotten a call from Ms. Dobbins, the lady who ran the animal shelter where Lizzie volunteered. Since the Petersons were known for fostering puppies, taking in young dogs who needed homes, Ms. Dobbins knew just where to turn when she had a puppy she couldn't keep at the shelter. Charles's older sister knew more about dogs than most adults. She had begged Mom to let her stay home and foster the "emergency puppy."

"Mom may not be so happy about the situation, either," Dad said. "She was looking forward to a weekend on her own, when she could really enjoy visiting with her friends."

It was Mom's annual reunion weekend, when she got together with three friends from college. One year she had gone all the way to California to see "the girls," but this year they were all coming to Littleton. Mom had been cleaning the house for weeks and had even bought new curtains for the living room.

"Hey," Dad said. "Forget about Lizzie and the puppy. Let's just have a fantastic boys' weekend, okay? You, me, Buddy, and the Bean. Boys rule!"

Charles had to smile. "Boys rule!" he repeated, looking back at the Bean, happy in his car seat, and at Buddy, curled up peacefully on his soft doggy bed in the way-back.

Buddy was the only foster puppy the Petersons had kept forever. Charles loved him so much, from the tip of his waggy tail to the top of his adorable nose. What could be better than a camping trip with his best pal? Charles sat up straighter in his seat. "How big is this campground, anyway?" he asked.

"I don't know," Dad admitted. "I found it online, and I arranged everything with a few phone calls. The people who run it seem very nice."

"And it has a lake?" Charles asked.

"A lake, and streams, and woods. And I bet there won't be many people there at all, since the nights are getting cold lately."

"What kind of fish are we going to catch?" Charles asked.

"Well, I don't know. Maybe some bass or a big toothy pike." Dad flashed his teeth at Charles and chomped noisily.

"If I catch a pike, you're taking it off the line," Charles said. He did not like the idea of a big toothy fish.

"Pike!" yelled the Bean. "Pike smike like trike!"

They all cracked up.

"Hey, is this it?" Charles pointed to another sign. "Finster Family Campground?"

"This is it!" Dad said, turning onto an unpaved road. "The man I spoke to — Mr. Finster, I guess — said to grab a map from the front porch at the lodge, then go straight on to our campsite."

He pulled the van up to a big brown log cabin with green shutters. "This must be the lodge — and there's a box with the maps in it," he said. "Hop out and grab one, will you?"

Charles unbuckled and got out of the van. He took a long, deep breath of the piney-smelling air. Its freshness washed away all the sleepiness and grumpiness he had been feeling. Suddenly, he couldn't wait to see the lake and their campsite. He trotted up the broad wooden steps to the wide porch, noticing the green wooden rocking chairs placed all along its length, and pulled a map out of the box labeled CAMPGROUND MAPS. Next to it was a glass case that held a typewritten sheet titled, "Finster Family News and Views." A quick glance told him that it covered campground news, like the weather and the largest fish someone had caught in the past week. It even had a special feature about bats. There was also a column called "Stella's Story," headed by a blurry picture of a small white dog. Charles stepped up to take a closer look, but just then Dad beeped the horn.

"We'd better keep moving if we want to get ourselves set up before dark," he called.

Charles got into the van and passed the map to Dad.

Dad passed it back. "You navigate. Our campsite is the one called Elm. Tell me which way to go."

Charles bent over the hand-drawn map and puzzled out the route to their campsite. "Take a right up there," he said, pointing to a fork in the road just past the lodge. "I think."

Soon they passed the lake — more of a pond, really, but big enough, and almost as blue as the one in the painting on the sign — and wound their way along a twisty road lined with tall pines. "Maple, Oak, Spruce . . ." Charles read the sign in front of each empty campsite they passed. He wondered if they were the *only* campers at the Finster Family Campground. "There it is. Elm!"

"Well done," said Dad, swinging the van into the flat, sandy campsite. Charles saw a shelter with three walls and a roof, a fire pit made from a ring of stones, and a picnic table. He unbuckled the Bean's car seat and they all got out and stretched. "Ah," said Dad. "Smell that air! This is going to be great. No computers, no cell phone service, just men in nature. What could be better than that?"

Buddy sniffed the air, too. Then he shook himself off and wandered over to a tall pine to lift his leg.

"Where do *we* go to the bathroom?" Charles asked Dad. Not that he had to go right then. He just wanted to know.

Dad pointed to a building, and Charles saw a path to it through the woods. "That's probably where we get water, too," said Dad. "The Bean and I can go check. Why don't you take that broom" — he pointed to a broom leaning against a tree — "and sweep out our lean-to so we can set our things up in a clean area." He pointed to the three-sided shelter.

Charles hitched Buddy's leash to the picnic table and helped Dad unload the big cooler and the camp stove. Then, while Dad and the Bean headed off to get water, he began to sweep pine needles and sand out of the lean-to, pausing now and then to sniff the fresh air and crane his neck for a glimpse of the lake, which glittered and glistened through the trees.

When he heard Buddy whine, he figured Dad and the Bean must have returned. He poked his head out of the lean-to, ready to ask if they'd found water — but they weren't there. Instead, he saw Buddy in the middle of a play bow, front legs splayed out in front and bottom in the air. And bowing back, as if to say, "Sure, I'd love to play!" was the cutest, fluffiest little white dog Charles had ever seen.

CHAPTER TWO

"Hey, who are you?" Charles asked, hopping down out of the lean-to. Both dogs ignored him as they sniffed each other, wagging their tails. Charles felt his heart thumping. Was this a runaway puppy? Maybe a dog he could foster? That would show Lizzie, wouldn't it? She wasn't the only one who knew how to help puppies. He edged closer to the dogs, trying to see whether the small white pup was wearing a collar with tags on it. She was so cute. She looked like a stuffed animal, with perky ears, a fluffy tail, and shiny black eyes almost hidden behind a fringe of white hair.

"Stella!" yelled someone with a voice that

sounded like a croaky frog's. A moment later, Charles saw two old people walk into their campsite. The man was tall and thin, but he stooped over his wooden cane. The woman was short and round, with silvery hair all frizzed out around her happy pink face.

The dogs ignored them and kept on playing. Now Buddy had found a big, gnarled stick. He teased the other dog with it, prancing in front of her with the stick in his mouth.

Look what I have! It's a very, very special stick. Don't you want it?

Before Charles could figure out what to say to the couple, Dad stepped into the clearing along with the Bean. He carried two jugs full of water. "Oh, hello," he said. "You must be our hosts."

"Eh?" said the man.

"What'd he say?" said the woman.

"Are you the Finsters?" Dad asked, a little louder.

The man nodded and smiled. "Frank and Beansie Finster, at your service," he croaked.

"Nice to meet you, Frank." Dad stepped up to him and stuck out his hand, but the man just laughed. "She's Frank," he said, pointing to the woman. "My lovely bride of fifty years, Frances Finster. And everybody calls me Beansie. Don't ask why."

"Why?" Charles couldn't help asking. The man didn't seem to hear him, but he answered anyway.

"Well, I guess I got that name because I love beans. Always have. Navy beans, pinto beans, white beans, green beans. Lima beans, pork 'n' beans, any kind of beans. I'm crazy about 'em, and Frank here cooks 'em better than anybody. Guess that's why we're still married after all these years."

The Bean was excited. He jumped up and down next to Charles. "I'm the Bean," he sang. "I'm the Bean."

The man didn't seem to hear him, either. He just looked up at the sky, listing more beans he liked as he ticked them off on his fingers. "I can go for a soldier bean," he mused. "Or a rattlesnake bean. That's a good one, too. And of course Frank makes a mean pot of Boston baked beans, seeing as how her folks are originally from down that way. . . ."

The Bean ran over and tugged at his sleeve until the man looked down at him. "I'm the Bean," he said.

"Eh?" the man asked.

"What'd he say?" the woman asked, peering at the Bean.

"Black beans, red beans and rice, even a jelly bean — you show me a bean and I'm gonna eat it up." Beansie was unstoppable.

The Bean shrieked. "Don't eat me!"

Frank and Beansie heard that. They stared at the Bean, their mouths open in surprise.

"This is our youngest, Adam." Dad spoke extra loudly — almost shouting — so Charles knew his dad had probably figured it out, too: The Finsters were a little bit hard of hearing. "We call him the Bean."

Beansie Finster grinned. "Well then, I guess I'll probably like you just as well as any other bean, won't I?" He ruffled the Bean's hair as he looked around the campsite. "Y'all just got here, I guess. Stella must have figured that out before we did." He nodded at the little white dog. "Isn't she cute as a button? We just got her this spring. She's a handful, though." He shook his head, and his wife shook hers, too, making a *tsk, tsk* sound. "She just doesn't listen."

Stella and Buddy tore around the campsite, first chasing one way, then the other, kicking up pinecones and leaping over the fire pit.

"Stella's a Maltipoo, a cross between a Maltese and a miniature poodle. Our kids gave her to us for an anniversary present," said Frank. "We've always had dogs here at the campground, haven't we, Beansie?"

Beansie nodded. "They live with us in our RV when we go south," he said. "They're snowbirds, just like us."

"Snowbirds?" Charles asked.

Dad put a hand on Charles's shoulder. "That means they go to Florida or somewhere else warm for the winter," he explained.

Beansie barely seemed to notice them talking. He looked at Stella, who lay panting in the dirt next to Buddy. The two dogs had tired each other out. Beansie called Stella. "Come on, girl," he croaked. "I know you like to visit, but it's time to let these people get on with their unpacking."

Stella didn't move. Was she too tired? Or was she ignoring Beansie on purpose? "Come on, Stella," Charles said, catching her eye. He bent down and patted his knees. "Come here, girl."

Stella got up, trotted right to Charles, and sat down to let him clip on her leash. Charles was surprised. "She does listen sometimes," he said.

"Eh?" asked Beansie.

"What'd he say?" asked Frank.

Dad grinned. "He said that Stella is a good girl," he hollered.

Beansie shook his head. "Maybe not good enough," he said. "She's going to have to learn to behave before we leave for St. Pete. We can't have her running all over the trailer park down there."

"No," agreed Frank. "The old folks wouldn't like it."

Beansie gave Dad a little salute. "Stop by later and we'll talk about boats and fishing and all that. And if you forgot anything — like some bait worms or maybe an ice cream sandwich, say — you might just find it at the camp store."

Dad and Charles grinned at each other as Frank and Beansie headed off, with Stella trotting along next to them. "What a couple of characters!" Dad said. "I have a feeling this place is going to be a lot of fun."

CHAPTER THREE

Dad looked at the sky and Charles followed his glance. The sun was sliding down over the tops of the pine trees, and there was a pinkish glow in the direction of the lake. "We'd better finish unloading if we want to get our camp set up by dark," said Dad.

Charles followed his father to the van and let him load up his arms with stuff: air mattresses, a flashlight, his school backpack filled with the clothes he would need. He couldn't stop thinking about Stella. Wow, was she adorable. She reminded Charles of Snowball, a little West Highland white terrier his family had once fostered. Her curly white hair was longer and silkier than Snowball's, and she was smaller, but she had the same wavy tail and funny, furry face. Charles had a feeling she was smart, even though she didn't always behave. She could walk nicely on her leash, and she had come when he had called her. She was just curious. Of course she would want to check out any new people who came to her campground.

He dumped his armload into the lean-to, where the Bean sat curled up cozily in a sleeping bag, and went back for more. This time Dad handed him a small cooler, a bag of groceries that felt like it weighed about eighty pounds, and Buddy's food bowl. "What's for dinner tonight?" Charles asked.

Dad laughed. "Funny you should ask," he said. "We happen to be having beans. Chili, that is."

"Yum," said Charles. Chili was one of Dad's specialties. He had learned how to make it from another firefighter at the firehouse where he worked. "Maybe we should invite Beansie and Frank."

"Great minds think alike," Dad said.

"Eh?" asked Charles, feeling a bit like Frank.

"Just a saying," said Dad. "It means that I had the same idea. Get it? I'm saying how brilliant we both are."

Charles shrugged. He didn't exactly get it, but it didn't matter. If Frank and Beansie came to dinner, that meant Stella would, too. He bent down to pet Buddy as he passed the spot where his pup was tied up. "Maybe you'll get to see your new friend again soon," he said.

Dad handed Charles another load out of the van. "How much stuff did we bring, anyway?" Charles asked. "I never knew camping was so complicated." When he had camped in his friend David's backyard, all they'd had was a tent and

20

two sleeping bags. They had set the whole thing up in about ten minutes.

"It just takes a little more effort if you want to be comfortable," said Dad. "You'll thank me later." He climbed out of the van, carrying the tent bag and a hammer. "Trust me, we'll have the best campsite ever when we're done."

First Charles and Dad set up the tent. Dad put the poles together while Charles hammered the stakes into the sandy soil. Once their little house was upright, they made their beds by blowing up air mattresses and laying out sleeping bags and pillows. Dad hung a flashlight from a loop inside the tent and tucked the keys to the van into a pocket near the zippered door. "Looks good, doesn't it?" he said.

Charles and the Bean both lay on their sleeping bags, testing out their new beds. "Comfy," Charles admitted. In fact, it was so comfy that he almost wished he could take a nap, like he used to when he was the Bean's age.

"Great," Dad said, brushing off his hands. "Now, let's get our kitchen set up."

Charles groaned. There sure was a lot of work to do when you went camping. At least he would earn a badge or two for Cub Scouts. He followed Dad to the picnic table and helped organize things so they'd be easy to find once it got dark. Then Dad asked Charles and the Bean to pick up all the sticks they could find in their campsite and in the empty campsites on either side. "We'll need kindling for our fire," he said.

Charles had just loaded up his arms when he saw a white blur zip past him, toward the picnic table. Stella! She was back. By the time he got to the fire pit, Stella and Buddy were wrestling under the table. "Stella," Charles called, but she ignored him as she and Buddy twisted and tumbled. Her feathery tail wagged with joy at finding Buddy again.

Hey, friend! I was wondering if you were still here.

Dad looked at the two dogs and sighed. "Maybe you'd better take her back to the lodge," he said. "You can take Buddy for a walk at the same time. I hate to leave him tied up so long. And don't forget to invite Beansie and Frank to dinner."

Charles found a piece of rope to use as a leash for the little white puppy and tied one end to her collar. Stella stood still once she knew what he wanted, looking up at him with shiny black eyes. It was funny how sometimes she totally ignored his commands and other times she behaved just perfectly. "Good girl," he said, smiling at her and reaching down to ruffle her fur. She smiled back, showing her little pink tongue, and wagged her tail.

I love making new friends!

Charles walked down the camp road with the two puppies. They pulled in opposite directions, sniffing at every tree and bush along the way. "Come on, you two," said Charles, laughing. He knew that every smell was brand-new for Buddy, so he tried to be patient.

Back at the lodge, Charles stopped on the porch to take a closer look at the Finster Family News and Views — especially the part titled "Stella's Story." It was funny, a column written from Stella's point of view about her wanderings through the campground, her meeting with a duck one day, and her opinions about everything from beetles ("Crunchy, but not very flavorful") to firewood ("I love the smell of birch logs burning, don't you?").

"Well, look who's here," said Frank, opening the screen door wide. "And look who you've brought home." She shook her head at Stella.

"I came to ask you and Beansie to dinner," Charles said, practically shouting it so he could be sure Frank would hear him. "We're having chili."

"Beansie will be happy to hear that." Frank looked down at Stella. "Stella, go find Beansie!" she said, gesturing with two open palms. "Where's Beansie?" Stella dashed off into the cabin and Frank laughed. "She loves that game."

A moment later, Stella raced back, with Beansie following her. When Frank told him why Charles was there, Beansie grinned. "Chili! One of my favorite ways to eat beans. It's a date, and we'll bring some of Frank's famous lemon bars for dessert," he said. "As a matter of fact, we had something to ask you, too." He bent to pet Stella's soft white curls, then slowly straightened up again. "We saw the way Stella came when you called. You have a real way with dogs. And it made us think — well, we were wondering if you might be able to help us look after our girl."

CHAPTER FOUR

"Charles told me you asked about whether we could help out with Stella," Dad said as he passed bowls of chili to Beansie and Frank. They all sat around the picnic table, with Stella and Buddy lying at their feet, as darkness fell and the stars came out. A crackling fire warmed Charles's front, while his back was cooled by the night air. He liked that feeling. In a minute, he'd stand with his back to the fire, just to switch things up.

"Eh? Oh, yes. Well, it's just that . . . well, you seem like awfully nice people," said Frank. "And then I saw how good Charles was with Stella, and with your own dog. So I said to Beansie, I said, 'Why not ask them?'"

"We *are* nice," said Charles, looking right at Frank. Dad had told him that it would be easier for Frank and Beansie to hear him if he made sure they were looking straight at his face while he spoke. "Plus, we're a foster family. We have lots of experience with puppies." He explained how their family had taken care of all kinds of dogs who had needed help.

"See?" Frank nudged Beansie. "I knew they were perfect."

"Well, isn't that something?" croaked Beansie. "Isn't that just the bee's knees?" He reached for another piece of corn bread and spread butter thickly on top of it. "The thing is, we're not as young as we used to be. Every year about this time we start closing up the campground so we're ready to skedaddle before the snow starts flying.

You know, we turn off the water pipes and tidy everything up, and put the picnic tables under cover, clean up the trails and campsites, and . . ." He looked tired just talking about it. "Anyway, it seems to take longer every year, especially now that our kids are grown and live far away."

"It sounds like a lot of work," Dad said.

"It is," said Frank. "And now this one" — she nodded down at Stella, under the table — "is making it even harder. We've always been able to let our campground dogs roam free around here. It's safe, back on this dead-end road. But Stella keeps running off where we can't see her, and she doesn't come when we call, and if we tie her up, she cries like a baby and it breaks my heart to hear it."

"Aww," said Charles.

"Aww," echoed the Bean. Charles saw him sneak a piece of corn bread down to the puppies, but luckily none of the adults did. Charles slipped

Buddy and Stella another chunk as soon as he had the chance.

"Well," Dad said. "I know Charles and the Bean would love to have Stella around, and she and Buddy seem to be getting along very well. We'd be happy to help out."

Charles and the Bean grinned at each other. A new foster puppy! What could be better?

Charles felt content as he snuggled down into his sleeping bag that night. Dad and the Bean were sleeping right nearby in the tent, his tummy was full of delicious food, and best of all, they had a new puppy to take care of.

He closed his eyes, and when he opened them, it was morning. Barely. Dad shook Charles's shoulder as soon as the first light of day seeped into the tent. "Better get up, chief," he said. "Those bass are going to be biting down at the lake."

Charles groaned. He'd almost forgotten that they had planned to get up early each morning to go fishing. The plan had sounded good at the time — before he found out how cold the mornings would be. He snuggled down deeper into his sleeping bag, but then Buddy started to lick his face, and the Bean began to whine about having to go pee, and Dad kept coming into and going out of the tent, zipping and unzipping the door. Who could sleep with all that going on? He climbed out of his bag, stuck his feet into his sneakers, and helped the Bean pull on his sweatshirt. "Let's go," he said, leading his little brother to the bathrooms.

By the time they got back, Dad had some bacon sizzling in a pan and the picnic table was set for breakfast, with cereal, juice, and milk. "Eat up," said Dad as he poured out some dog food for Buddy. "Then we'll head down to the lake. I feel lucky today, don't you?" He rubbed his hands together to keep them warm.

"Is Stella coming with us?" Charles asked. He couldn't wait to spend more time getting to know the fluffy white pup.

Dad shook his head. "Two dogs in a canoe might be too much to handle. I told Frank and Beansie that we'd come get her after we went fishing."

Beansie had promised that a canoe and paddles would be waiting for them at the dock. Charles knew that Dad had his eye on a fishing spot he'd seen across the small lake, where lily pads floated on the surface of the water. Dad had asked about it the night before, and Frank had told him that he was right about that place. "You'll catch some bass there for sure," she'd said.

When the breakfast dishes were done, they trooped down to the lake. Sure enough, a canoe was tied to the dock, all set to go, with life jackets and paddles nearby. Charles helped the Bean into his jacket, then put on his own with help from Dad. "What about Buddy?" Charles asked. "Doesn't he need a life jacket?"

"Good point," said Dad. "Luckily, Frank said this lake is very shallow, and Buddy is a pretty good swimmer. I think we'll be fine." He helped the Bean into the canoe, then Charles. "Okay, Buddy," he called. "Let's hop in."

Usually when someone said that, like when they were near the van, Buddy knew just what to do. But he did not seem to want to "hop in" to the canoe. Instead, he ran up and down the dock, whining. He wanted to be with Charles and the Bean — that was clear — but he did not like the idea of getting into a tippy, floating boat. "C'mon, Buddy," called Charles. "You can do it."

But he couldn't — or wouldn't. No matter how hard they tried to convince him, Buddy would not get into the canoe.

Dad squinted at the spot with the water lilies. Then he sighed and helped Charles and the Bean out of the canoe. "I guess we'll just fish off the dock today," he said. "We'll want to use worms instead of lures, though. How about if the Bean and I stay here and get us all set up while you run to the lodge for some bait?"

Charles took off his life jacket and trotted up the hill to the lodge, wondering if there would be a new installment of "Stella's Story" posted with the Finster Family News and Views. Sure enough, there was — and it was all about him and his family!

Had dinner with my new friend, Buddy, and his people, two very nice boys and their dad. Our only guests at the campground right now, but we're happy to have them. Terrific corn bread! it said.

Charles smiled. Frank and Beansie might not hear very well, but they didn't miss much.

Beansie was happy to sell Charles a small container of worms — and even happier when Charles said he might as well take Stella with him right then, since they'd just be fishing off the dock. "Stella," Beansie croaked over his shoulder. "Your friend is here for you."

Charles could see Stella snoozing on a rag rug, right behind Beansie.

"Stella," Beansie croaked again. The puppy kept sleeping. Finally, Beansie turned, bent down, and nudged her on the shoulder. "Let's go, girl," he said. Stella popped awake and jumped to her feet, ready for action.

Charles knelt down and Stella pranced happily into his arms.

Hi, friend!

She licked his face and he could smell her sweet puppy breath. "Good girl," he said. "Want to come with me?" He kissed the top of her head, wondering how the puppy could have slept through Beansie's shouts. Cute as she was, there was something about Stella that had been bothering Charles. Then, suddenly, he thought he might know what it was.

Maybe Stella had something in common with her owners.

Something to do with her hearing.

CHAPTER FIVE

Stella was small, but she was fast. She kept right up with Charles as he trotted back to the dock. He held her leash in one hand and a plastic container of worms in the other. Beansie and Charles had agreed that it would be a good idea to keep Stella on a leash for a while. Charles knew that it was a big responsibility to take care of someone else's dog.

The lake was still and quiet when Charles got to the dock. Bits of mist were rising over the hillside of pointy-topped pine trees on the far shore. From the map, Charles knew that there was a trail that went all around the lake. It went to some far-off campsites, for people who didn't mind hiking farther into the woods.

Dad had their rods ready: The Bean's was only a plastic toy with no real hook, but Charles got to use a beautiful old rod that had been his father's when Dad was a kid. It had a cork handle, worn smooth where Dad had held it over the years.

"Got the worms? Great," said Dad. He reached for the container and Charles handed it over, glad that his father would take care of putting the worms on their hooks. That was one part of fishing Charles had never liked. Maybe someday he would get used to it, but for now he was happy to let Dad pick up the moist, squirmy worm and stick the sharp hook through its belly. Ugh.

While Dad baited their hooks and the Bean watched his red plastic bobber float on the glassy surface of the lake, Charles turned to Stella. She was gazing straight back up at him. Would she hear him if he gave her a command? "Sit," he said. She kept looking at him, her head cocked.

I think you want me to do something, but I'm not sure what it is.

Maybe she didn't know that one. Charles tried another command. "Lie down," he said, moving his palm toward the dock. Instantly, Stella lay down. She looked at Charles, happily thumping her tail.

That one's easy. When I can see your hand move, I know just what to do.

Buddy lay down next his new friend and the two started to wrestle. Dad nudged Charles and handed him his rod, with the hook baited and ready to go. "I've been seeing some fish rise over that way,"

Dad said, pointing to the left, where some reeds waved above the water.

Charles knew what "rising" meant. When a fish came up to grab an insect to eat, it would sometimes make a splash and leave widening circles on the surface of the lake. He looked toward the reeds and got ready to cast his line as far as possible in that direction. First he made sure that the dogs were out of the way and Stella's leash was still securely tied to one of the dock's posts.

When he looked at them, both puppies jumped up, as if it were time to play. "Uh-uh," said Charles. "Sit."

Obediently, Buddy sat. Stella didn't. Her attention was not on Charles now; it was on a duck that happened to be swimming by, trailing three baby ducks behind her. The baby ducks paddled like mad, cheeping in high voices as they tried to keep up with their mom.

"Ducks!" yelled the Bean. "Quack, quack!"

"Stella," called Charles. The puppy did not turn around. Was it because she was paying attention to the ducks — or because she couldn't hear him?

When the ducks finally swam out of sight, Stella looked up at Charles. He smiled at her. "Down," he said, moving his hand toward the dock. Stella lay down. Charles bent over to pet her and scratch her between the ears. How well did those perky white ears work, anyway?

"Dad," Charles said as they stood next to each other on the dock, their fishing lines dangling in the water. "I think there might be something wrong with Stella's hearing."

Dad looked at him. "Why do you say that?" he asked. "She seems fine to me."

"I've just been noticing things," Charles said. "Like she only obeys me if she's looking at me when I tell her to do something. You know, like

Frank and Beansie only hear us well when they're looking at us?"

Dad nodded. "You're very observant, Charles. I mean you're good at noticing things. But I hope you're wrong about this." He looked at Stella, who was facing away from them. "Stella," he called. Then "Stella!" he called again, a little louder. He snapped his fingers. "Stella!" Now he was almost shouting.

Charles watched Stella closely. She didn't jump up or look around or cock her head. Her ears didn't even twitch. "See?" he asked Dad.

Dad clapped his hands loudly.

This time Stella did turn.

"She seemed to hear that," Dad said. "Maybe she's not completely deaf."

For the rest of the morning, they spent more time on Stella than they did on fishing. Their rods lay forgotten on the dock as they jingled coins, made kissy noises, and tried different hand signals, trying to figure out how much Stella could hear and understand.

When Frank and Beansie came to see if they'd caught anything, Dad shook his head. "But there's something you should know," he told them. "We think there's something wrong with Stella's hearing."

Frank squinted at him. "Eh?" she said.

"What'd he say?" asked Beansie.

CHAPTER SIX

At first they didn't believe it. "She's just a naughty little girl sometimes, that's all," said Frank after Charles and Dad explained more about why they thought Stella's hearing might not be very good.

"She's a puppy," said Beansie. "Just a baby. You can't expect her to be perfect." He scooped Stella into his arms, and he and Frank both smiled down at her. Frank rubbed Stella's belly, and Beansie kissed her fluffy ears. "Just a little baby puppy, that's all," he croaked softly.

"Maybe if you just let your vet check her out . . ." Charles began, but Dad put a hand on his shoulder to shush him. It was pretty clear that Frank and Beansie were not listening.

They were not listening — but it turned out that they had heard him. Later that afternoon, while the Bean napped and Dad cut up onions for that night's beef stew, Charles was playing with Buddy and Stella, tossing a ball of rolled-up socks for them to run after. Stella was good at getting the socks, but not quite as good at bringing them back. Often she ran away with them, tossing her head in victory, proud of her prize. Charles was chasing her down when Beansie strolled into their campsite and cleared his throat.

"Like to come along on a couple of errands with me?" he asked Charles. "It's time to take Miss Amanda out for a test ride."

"Miss Amanda?" asked Charles.

"Our Airstream trailer," explained Beansie. "The one we live in all winter. That's what we call her, after Frank's grandma. I just hitched her up to my truck, and I like to be sure that everything's working right before we head south." He kicked at the dirt. "And also, I thought we might take Stella with us and swing by Doc Oliver's office. That's her vet."

Charles stopped chasing after Stella and the sock ball. "Oh," he said.

Beansie nodded. "We thought about what you said, and we talked about it while we cleaned up the volleyball court and the horseshoe pit. Frank and I agree. It can't hurt to get Stella checked out."

Charles grinned. "That's great," he said. "Dad, can I go?"

A half hour later, Beansie pulled up to their campsite in his big green pickup. Hitched behind the truck was a long, sleek silver trailer.

"Wow," said Charles. "Is that Miss Amanda?"

"Come on, I'll give you the tour," said Beansie. He opened the door and showed Charles, Dad, and the Bean inside. "See? We have everything we need in here."

Charles looked around. He had never seen such a cozy place. There was a tiny kitchen with a tiny stove and a tiny sink with a window above it. There was a small table near a larger window. Red-and-white checked curtains gave the trailer a homey look. A bed with a red-and-white quilt was tucked into the front of the trailer, and in the back was a tiny bathroom, with a shower and everything. Beansie showed them the built-in cabinets for dishes and food and clothes and books, opening the doors so they could see how neatly everything was put away. "Frank has this place set up just so," he said. "She makes sure it's a real home for us." He pointed to the cushioned seat by the table. "That's Stella's favorite spot."

Charles was in love. He wanted to live in a trailer just like this. How cool would it be to have everything you needed within reach, and to be able to drive anywhere and have your home right there with you? "Can I ride back here?" he asked. He didn't want to leave the cozy space.

Beansie shook his head. "Sorry, Skeezix. I need you up front with me, in the truck. Stella can sit on your lap."

Right, Stella. Charles had almost forgotten all about their real errand. He followed Beansie out of the trailer and climbed into the passenger seat of the truck. "See you," he called, waving to his dad and brother as Stella settled herself on his lap.

Once they'd left the campground's bumpy dirt roads, the truck glided smoothly along. Charles looked back to see Miss Amanda riding easily behind them. "Does Stella like to be in the trailer?" he asked, speaking loudly so Beansie could hear him over the noise of the truck.

"Well, we only got her this spring, so she hasn't spent a whole winter with us in there — but so far she seems to think it suits her just fine," Beansie said. "She jumps in there whenever one of us opens the door." He smiled fondly at the puppy in Charles's lap. "Mainly I think she just likes to be around people."

Soon Beansie pulled the truck and trailer up in front of a big ramshackle house that was painted bright blue. PETER OLIVER, VETERINARIAN read a sign out front. "Well," said Beansie, looking at Stella, "I suppose we'd better go in and see what the doc thinks."

Doc Oliver was almost as old as Frank and Beansie. He had a friendly smile and his blue eyes, behind wire-rimmed glasses, were kind. "Beansie, good to see you again," he said when his assistant, Mary, led them into the exam room. "And this sweetie-pie puppy of yours. She's not already due for booster shots, is she?" He bent down to pick up Stella and set her on his exam table.

"Well, no, she's not," said Beansie. "Charles here — he's a guest at our campground, and he and his dad have been helping out with Stella — well, Charles and his dad think that maybe Stella's a bit hard of hearing."

Doc Oliver straightened up and looked over his glasses at Charles. "Is that so?" he asked. "Tell me why you think that."

Charles explained that Stella seemed to obey commands only if she was looking at him — and, even then, only if he made a hand motion. "She doesn't hear you if you call her when she's not looking," he said. "Even if you yell."

"Is there some kind of test you can give her?" Beansie asked.

Doc Oliver looked thoughtful. "The only real test for deafness in dogs is pretty fancy and expensive. But it's usually fairly easy to tell if a dog can't hear." He asked Charles to keep Stella's attention while Doc Oliver walked around behind her. Then the doctor snapped his fingers, jingled some keys, and called her name.

Stella's ears did not twitch once.

Doc Oliver clapped his hands loudly. This time, Stella turned to look at him.

"See?" Beansie asked eagerly. "She can hear."

Doc Oliver shook his head. "I'm afraid not," he said. "She sensed the vibrations of my clapping, but I don't believe she heard anything else I did. I think your young friend is right. I think Stella is deaf."

CHAPTER SEVEN

Beansie stared at Doc Oliver. He did not say "Eh?" or "What'd he say?" Doc Oliver must have been used to Beansie, because he spoke loudly enough for the old man to hear.

But Charles could hardly believe what he was hearing, even though it was what he had suspected all along. "Really? Stella is deaf?"

"I'm afraid so," said Doc Oliver. "From the things you've told me and what I've seen . . . well, it's pretty clear." He stroked Stella's ears.

"But — why? I mean, why did she go deaf?" Charles reached out to pet Stella, too. How could this happen to such a sweet little puppy? Stella wagged her tail, just the tiniest wag, and looked up at him with her shiny black eyes.

Why is everyone so serious all of a sudden?

"She was probably born deaf, and has learned to make her way in the world by watching carefully," Doc Oliver said. "It's not as unusual as you might think. Many animals with a white coat — cats *and* dogs — have problems with their hearing."

Charles looked at Beansie. So far, he had not said a word. The old man's lips were a straight line, and his face was pale. Then he finally spoke. "We've had white dogs before," he croaked. "They could all hear perfectly well."

Doc Oliver nodded. "Of course. Not all white dogs are deaf. But many deaf dogs are white, or partly white. Like Dalmatians, for example. It's not at all unusual to meet a deaf Dalmatian."

Beansie was still pale, Charles noticed, and he had not stepped forward to pet Stella. He shook his head. "The poor little thing," he said. "How am I going to tell Frank? She loves this pup so much."

Doc Oliver smiled. "It's not the worst thing in the world," he said, his hand on Stella's head. "Deaf dogs can get along perfectly well, with a lot of love and a little help."

"How do we help Stella?" Charles tried to ignore the way Beansie was shaking his head. "What do we have to do? I'll do anything."

Doc Oliver crossed his arms and looked down at Charles. "Well," he began, "you'd need to teach her some hand signals so she understands what you expect of her."

"She already knows the one for 'lie down.'" Charles showed Doc Oliver the sign he'd used with Stella. "She's so smart, really. I know she can learn fast."

Doc Oliver nodded. "Deaf dogs can surprise you. My assistant, Mary, has two deaf dogs. She has taught them so much. She uses a combination of the hand signs many dog trainers use, plus some American Sign Language. You know, the language used by deaf people? I'm sure she could help you learn."

"Cool," said Charles. He glanced at Beansie, hoping for a smile. But Beansie did not look convinced. Charles turned back to the vet. "Can her dogs do tricks and stuff?"

"Sure," said Doc Oliver. "They know how to sit and shake and roll over and all that — but they also know the signs for things like 'get off the couch' and 'want to go for a walk?'"

Charles looked down at Stella. When most dogs heard the word "walk," they perked right up. Stella didn't even move her head. She really was deaf. He was still getting used to the idea, so he could imagine how hard it would be for Beansie, her owner, to understand.

"Does she have a habit of nipping a little too hard?" Doc Oliver asked. "Sometimes deaf puppies are like that, since they can't hear the squeals of their moms or littermates."

Charles remembered Chewy, a Chihuahua his family had once fostered. Chewy wasn't deaf, but he had not learned that it wasn't okay to bite hard. Charles had helped train him to stop by making sure to say "Ow!" out loud every time Chewy had nipped him.

"She used to." Beansie spoke up. "When we first got her, she used to bite my hands really hard. But I would give her just a little touch on the nose, and she learned to stop."

Doc Oliver nodded. "Deaf dogs can be quite sensitive to touch. It's a great way to give them praise, since they can't hear you say, 'Good dog.'

Some special petting will let her know she's done the right thing."

"What else?" Charles asked. "What else do we need to know about caring for a deaf puppy?" He ruffled Stella's ears and bent down so she could kiss his cheek. Maybe she was going to be fine after all.

"Let's see," said Doc Oliver. "It might be best to keep her on a leash when she's outdoors, just to be sure she's safe. She can't hear cars coming." He scratched his head. "Oh, and she may startle easily — jump up and maybe try to protect herself — if she's surprised when she's resting or sleeping. A gentle pat is a good way to let her know you're there."

Charles nodded. It didn't sound very hard. "Can you show us some more hand signals?" he asked. "Like for 'sit,' and 'come'?" Charles looked at Beansie. Why wasn't he joining in the discussion?

"Even better, why don't I ask Mary to come in and show you?" said Doc Oliver. "Let's see if she can give Stella her first lesson right now." He took Stella off the exam table and set her on the floor, then went to the door and called for Mary.

Charles looked at Beansie, hoping to see a smile. But Beansie was frowning at the floor. "What's the point?" he croaked. "We can't possibly keep this puppy. Doc, can't you just help us find her a new home?"

Doc Oliver raised his eyebrows. "Well . . . what if we at least try to train her first?"

Mary came in, smiling. "What's up?" she asked.

"It seems that Stella here is deaf," said Doc Oliver.

Mary nodded. "Well, I know from experience that it's not the end of the world," she said. "I'd be happy to help you learn how to help her."

Beansie's shoulders drooped. "I don't see how

we can do it," he said. "Frank and I? We can barely hear anything ourselves. Plus we've got the whole campground to take care of, and we can hardly keep up with that. We're a couple of old dogs, way too old to learn new tricks." He looked at the floor again, as defeated as a ballplayer who'd just struck out.

Charles couldn't stand to hear Beansie croaking out those sad words. "Can't we at least try?" he asked.

Beansie shrugged. "Go ahead," he said. "I'll wait outside." He stalked out of the office.

Mary and the vet looked at each other. "Some people really have a hard time with this," said Doc Oliver. "Some people even put deaf dogs to sleep."

Charles gulped. He knew what that meant, and he didn't even want to think about it. "Stella already knows the sign for 'lie down,'" he told Mary.

"Great. Let's start with that. Stella, lie down," she said, lowering her palm in front of her. Right away, Stella lay down, looking up at Mary hopefully.

I know that one!

"Good girl!" Mary gave Stella a big thumbs-up and reached into a nearby jar to grab a biscuit to give her. Stella jumped up and gobbled the treat. Mary held another treat over the puppy's head. "Now, sit," she said. She moved the treat backward so Stella had to look up to see it. Stella's eyes followed the treat, and as it moved, she sat. Mary gave her the treat with one hand while she raised the other, palm up, toward her own body. "That's the sign for 'sit,'" she told Charles. Then she gave Stella another thumbs-up. "What a good girl. She'll learn fast," said Mary.

"If only Beansie could learn fast, too," said Charles.

"Speaking of Beansie, tell him I'll send my daughter Emma over tomorrow to help at the campground. It sounds like they're swamped, and she's been looking for some part-time work," Mary said, smiling at Charles. "And don't worry. Stella is going to be just fine."

CHAPTER EIGHT

Charles told Beansie that Emma would be coming over, but besides that they didn't talk at all during the drive to the campground. When he pulled up to the Elm campsite, they sat in the truck for a moment without saying anything. Beansie had his hand on Stella's head, and he kept clearing his throat. When Charles started to say good-bye, Beansie picked up Stella and set her on Charles's lap. "You keep her from here on out," he said. "Find her a good home." His voice sounded even croakier than usual.

"But, Beansie —" Charles tried to think fast. How could he convince Beansie to change his mind?

Beansie interrupted him. "It's better this way," he said. "This is going to break Frank's heart. It's probably just best if she doesn't see much of Stella until you leave and take that puppy away with you."

Charles didn't know what to say — and he had a feeling that Beansie wouldn't listen to him anyway. Charles climbed out of the truck, cradling Stella in his arms. Beansie drove off without even saying good-bye.

Charles watched him go, wondering how Beansie could be so hard-hearted. He seemed like such a nice, gentle man — but now he was turning his back on one of the cutest, sweetest, smartest puppies in the world. Stella *needed* Frank and Beansie. Why couldn't Beansie understand that?

That night, Charles barely noticed what he was eating for dinner. He crawled into his sleeping bag before it even got dark, with Stella tucked in right beside him. He hugged her, wishing with all his might that he could help change Beansie's mind.

In the morning, she was still tucked in with him, all warm and sleepy and soft. "I guess you're really an official foster puppy now, Stella," Charles told her as he stroked her curly fur. Stella stretched and yawned, rolling onto her back for a tummy rub.

I miss my people, but you're pretty nice, too.

Dad had agreed that they could take care of Stella for the rest of their time at the campground — and take her home with them, too. "It won't be easy to find a home for a deaf dog, you know," he warned as he set out the breakfast things.

"Wait till you see what she can do when I train her," Charles told his dad. "Stella will be such a good puppy that anyone would want to adopt her." He tried to sound confident, but inside he couldn't help wondering if he'd ever find anyone who would love Stella as much as Frank and Beansie did. Why did Beansie have to be so stubborn?

Charles was finishing his cereal when he heard footsteps crunching on the gravel path toward their campsite. He turned to see Frank tiptoeing toward him, a finger over her lips. A brown-haired teenage girl walked along next to her. "This is Emma," Frank said. "Don't tell Beansie we came. He's got his mind made up, the stubborn old fool. He truly thinks it's the right thing for us to give Stella up. But I miss my little girl so much. I just had to see her." She knelt down and Stella scampered over to leap into her arms.

You came for me! Yay!

The puppy nuzzled Frank's cheeks, licking up the tears that spilled out of the old woman's eyes.

Charles felt his heart swell. It was obvious: Stella belonged with Frank and Beansie.

Emma must have thought so, too. "So does that mean you're going to keep her?" she asked. She reached out to pet Stella's soft curls.

Frank frowned and shook her head. "When Beansie makes up his mind, it stays made up. Especially with a decision as big as this one."

"Did he tell you about the hand signals?" Charles asked. "She's already learning fast." He showed Frank how the puppy lay down when he got her attention, then pushed his palm toward the floor. "See?" he asked.

Emma clapped her hands. "That's great," she said.

"Such a good girl," Frank sighed. "But Beansie is probably right about all that signal stuff being too much for us to deal with. It would be like learning a whole new language, and I can't imagine doing that at my age. It's hard enough dealing with this campground."

"But —" Emma started, then stopped.

Charles thought Frank looked tired — and sad.

Dad must have, too. He put a hand on Frank's arm. "If you really want us to find Stella a good home, that's what we'll do. We've done it for lots of other puppies, and we can do it for her. We just want you to be sure."

Charles looked at Emma. Would she and her mother, Mary, be interested in a third deaf dog? Then he shook his head sadly. Even a great home like that would not be the best home for Stella. She belonged with Frank and Beansie; he was sure of it.

Frank picked up Stella and bent her head to kiss the puppy's nose, and Charles caught a glimpse of another tear slipping down Frank's cheek. "We're sure," she said. Gently, she put Stella back on the ground and stood up. "We'd better get going," she said. "The day is slipping away and I've got all the bathrooms to clean. At least I'll have Emma to help me." She smiled at Emma, pulled a tissue out of her sleeve, and blew her nose. "By the way," she said when she was done. "We were going to offer to take care of Buddy today so you all could go fishing. Stella rides nicely in the canoe, so she can go with you."

Charles saw Dad's face light up. "Really? That would be terrific. I'm dying to try for those bass."

Frank nodded and reached for Buddy's leash. "What do you say, cutie?" she asked him. "Want to help Emma and ol' Frank today?"

Charles gave her a few of Buddy's treats and watched as his puppy pranced off happily with his new friends. "Frank loves dogs," he said.

Dad nodded. "It's a shame they can't keep Stella." He got up to clear the breakfast dishes. "I'll go wash these, and then we can head out in the canoe."

Charles and the Bean were playing "grab the sock" with Stella when the Bean looked up and started to laugh. "Beansie!" he shouted.

"Hush, my young friend," croaked Beansie with a finger over his lips, just like Frank. The old man walked into the campsite, raised his eyebrows at Charles, and whispered, "Don't tell Frank I was here." Then he squatted down and opened his arms, calling for Stella.

CHAPTER NINE

Later that morning, as he and his Dad started to get all their fishing gear together, Charles couldn't stop thinking about how Beansie had looked when he left their campsite. His droopy shoulders, his red-rimmed eyes: It was clear that Beansie was very sad and upset. So why didn't he just change his mind? Beansie had petted Stella and whispered to her, holding her up to his cheek and gazing into her black button eyes. Then he'd handed her to Charles. He cleared his throat. "Well, those fallen spruce trees on the Lake Trail aren't going to cut themselves up." He hoisted a big pack basket onto his back. "Hope the sound of

70

my chainsaw won't bother you too much," he croaked. Then he hiked off, headed for the trails on the far side of the lake.

"Why won't Beansie change his mind?" Charles asked his dad as they walked down to the lake. "He loves Stella as much as Frank does."

"I guess Frank is right about him being stubborn," Dad said. "He really does think that he's doing the right thing for Stella. He just doesn't believe that he and Frank can take care of her well enough."

"Well, he's wrong." Charles kicked at a pinecone. "Isn't he, Stella?" He looked down at the fluffy white puppy prancing by his side. She looked back at him and wagged her tail, opening her mouth in a sweet little doggy grin.

It was great to see my people this morning! I knew they still loved me.

Charles's throat closed up and he felt tears come to his eyes. Stella was the best. He gave her a thumbs-up. "Good girl," he said. "You're a good girl."

Stella really was a good girl. At the lake, she knew just what to do when Dad got the canoe positioned next to the dock: She jumped right in and settled herself in the very center of the boat. Charles helped the Bean get in; then he climbed carefully in himself. Finally, Dad climbed in and they paddled off, with Charles up front and Dad in back.

The air was crisp, but the sun was warm on Charles's shoulders. There wasn't another boat on the whole lake; it was like the day belonged to them. Charles dug his paddle into the water, stroking on one side and then on the other. His muscles hurt, but in a good way. He knew that his job was to keep the canoe moving through the water; Dad's job, in back, was to steer it.

They were halfway across the lake when Charles heard Beansie's chainsaw start up. Its loud whine echoed over the water. Charles turned to see if Stella heard anything, but she was looking the other way. He tried to see where Beansie was, but the trees grew too thickly on that side of the lake. From the map he knew that there was a lean-to over there called Aspen, which was on the Lake Trail near the rocky shore. He could see its roof, but not much else.

Dad steered them neatly into the little cove where the water lilies lay thick on the water's surface. Their round pads floated serenely, green against the blue of the lake. "Finally!" Dad said when they were floating amid the pads. "I just know this place is full of big bass."

Carefully, making sure to keep his weight centered so the canoe would not tip over, Charles turned around in his seat. Now he was facing his dad. Stella and the Bean, too. "Hi, good girl," he said, giving Stella a thumbs-up and a head scratch.

Dad handed the Bean his plastic rod, then opened his tackle box. "No more worms," he said. "For bass, we use these lures." He held up something that looked a bit like a gummy worm, with a hook attached. He passed Charles his rod, then got his own ready. "Look out, bass!" he said as he cast a line into the lily pads.

"Look out, bass," the Bean echoed, letting his own line droop over the canoe's side.

Charles cast his line and watched his bobber land between two lily pads. Then he sat up straight, watching it closely. If it moved even a little bit, he might have a bite. Charles and his dad always did catch-and-release fishing, which meant that after they caught a fish, they took the hook out and let it go, to swim and eat and grow even bigger. Charles knew Dad would talk him through what to do next, but he rehearsed the steps in his head anyway: First, it was good to land a fish — that is, catch it — as quickly as you could. Letting the fish fight for too long would tire it out, and it would not do as well when you let it go.

Next, it was important to keep the fish in the water. Instead of bringing it into the canoe, you should hold the fish in the water, maybe in a net, while you gently worked the hook out. Finally, you were supposed to hold the fish in the water for another moment, so it could recover, before you let it swim off. All of that was what you did *if* you caught a fish. So far, Charles wasn't even feeling a nibble.

"I got a bite!" yelled the Bean, happily jerking his rod all around. He loved to say that, even though no fish ever nibbled at his plastic hook.

"All right," said Dad. He scooped with the net, pretending to catch the fish on the Bean's line. "Wow! This guy must weigh a million pounds, at least."

The Bean laughed his googly laugh. "A billion gillion zillion!" he shouted.

Charles laughed, too. Then, suddenly, he stopped laughing. "Dad," he said. "I really do have a bite. And I think it's a big one." He watched the bobber sink and rise, sink and rise, as the fish tugged on the hook. His heart pounded.

Dad inched forward in the canoe, net in hand. "Reel him in slowly," he said. "Nice and even, that's right."

Charles saw the bobber moving toward him as he pulled in his line. Then he saw the fish. It slid through the water, shiny gray with a lighter cream-colored belly and as long as Charles's arm.

His heart beat even harder as the fish came closer.

"Nice one," said Dad. "Hey, what's that?" he cocked his head. "Do I hear yelling?"

Charles swiveled his head toward shore to listen. It was Frank's high voice calling Beansie's name. "Beansie! Where are you?" she yelled. Charles could see her, standing on the dock with Emma next to her.

Charles and Dad looked at each other, and Charles could tell that Dad was thinking the same thing he was. They had not heard Beansie's chainsaw for a while. Was the old man in trouble?

Dad squinted toward the dock. "They're getting into a canoe," he said. "Good idea. It's the quickest way to the other side of the lake." He helped Charles reel in the fish, then held it in the water while he worked the hook out quickly. After a moment, he let the fish swim off. Charles watched it go. That was the biggest fish he had ever caught, and he didn't even get to enjoy it.

Dad picked up his paddle. "Paddle hard! We'll meet up with them and get over there fast."

Charles turned around to face front again and dug his paddle into the lake's still waters, feeling the burn in his shoulders. The fish didn't matter at all, not if Beansie was in trouble. He watched the other canoe move toward them, closer and closer, until he could see Emma in the front, paddling even harder than he was paddling, and Frank in the back, steering them straight across the lake. Soon the two canoes were next to each other, moving quickly together toward the far shore and Aspen, the lean-to.

"I'm worried," Frank said to Dad. She was panting a little from the hard work of paddling. "I didn't notice the quiet until Emma mentioned it. But he expected to be working all day. He can't be finished yet. Why aren't we hearing the chainsaw?"

"We'll find him," Dad said. "Don't worry."

"We had to leave Buddy tied up at the dock," said Frank. "He just wouldn't get in the canoe. I'm so sorry."

Dad waved a hand. "The only thing that matters right now is finding Beansie. Buddy will be fine."

Moments later, Charles was jumping out of the canoe and helping pull it up onto a small, sandy beach. He helped the Bean and Stella climb out.

"Beansie!" Frank called as she stepped out of the other canoe with Emma's help. "Beansie, where are you?" Stella ran to her, and Frank bent to hug the small dog.

"Let's all yell together on the count of three," suggested Dad. "One . . . two . . . three."

"BEANSIE!" they all yelled.

Then they stood silently, listening. It was so quiet at the lake. Charles heard a bird chirping and the sound of a chipmunk rustling through leaves. He did not hear Beansie.

He looked at Stella. She looked up at him. "Stella," he said. "Can you find Beansie?"

Stella stared at him as if she did not understand.

Then Frank stepped up. "Find Beansie, Stella," she said. She held out both hands, palms up. "Where's Beansie?"

Stella's tail began to wag.

I know how to play this game!

The fluffy white puppy put her nose to the ground and sniffed. Then she began to run, pulling Charles after her. She scurried up the sandy beach so fast he could hardly keep up, hanging on to her leash. He looked back and saw that everyone was following them. The Bean seemed to think it was a game, too, but Dad and Frank and Emma looked very serious.

Stella dragged Charles up a dirt path that wound between two boulders and entered a forest of tall pines. There, in a clearing, lay Beansie — his leg trapped beneath a fallen tree.

CHAPTER TEN

STELLA'S STORY

Well, it sure has been exciting around here lately. You won't believe what happened yesterday.

It all started when I was out in the middle of the lake with my new friends, the two boys and their dad. There we were, peacefully floating along (I saw a turtle and three frogs), when all of a sudden things got crazy. Before I knew what was happening, our boat was moving so fast I could feel the wind in my ears. Next, another boat pulled up next to ours, and who do you think was in it? One of my people, my woman! I could tell right away that she was very upset about something, and I wanted to jump into her lap and comfort her, but the boy told me to lie down, so I did. I do like to please people. Plus, the boat got pretty tippy when I was trying to climb out.

Once I lay down, we started steaming along again, with my woman's boat keeping right up with ours. Then we came to the end of the water, and the boy hopped out to pull our boat onto the land. I hopped out, too. The other boat pulled up and my woman got out. She knelt down and held her arms open, and I ran right over to her and kissed her and kissed her and kissed her. She hugged me and put her face in my neck, and I could feel that her face was wet. What is that, anyway, when the salty water comes out of people's eyes? It always seems to happen when they are upset. Weird.

Finally, her eyes dried up (I helped by licking her cheeks) and she got to her feet. She gave me a very serious look and I wondered if I had done something wrong and she was going to tell me to go to my bed. But she didn't. Instead, she lifted her hands like she was asking me something. I knew what that meant! It's my favorite game of all, the one where I have to find the other person, my man. I'm really, really good at that game — at least when we're home. I know all the places he likes to hide. But we weren't in our house — we were in the woods. This was not going to be so easy. Lucky thing I like challenges.

I put my nose to the ground and sniffed. No man smell! I ran a few steps one way and sniffed again. Nothing. I ran the other way and sniffed so hard I thought my nose was going to fall off. I sniffed harder than I've ever sniffed in my entire life. I sniffed the ground, and then I sniffed the air, and then I sniffed the ground some more. Hmm. Maybe I smelled something. Maybe.

I ran a little farther and sniffed some more. Yes! Now I definitely smelled him. My man. I looked back to see if everyone was following me, and they were: the two boys, their father, my woman, and the nice girl who petted me. They were all running along behind me. What fun! How often do you get to play your favorite game and get chased all at the same time? I was in heaven.

I ran and ran, sniffing here and snuffling there. Now I had a good trail, and I knew my man was nearby. I ran over rocks and scooted under bushes. Even the prickly ones didn't bother me, because I knew I was getting closer. Then I burst into an open place with big tall trees all around. Right in the middle, one of the big tall trees was lying on its side — and under it lay my man! I ran right over to him and kissed him and kissed him and kissed him. Salty water came out of his eyes and he put out a hand to touch me, but he did not get up. He could not get up! That big tall tree was on his leg, trapping him.

I ran up and down, explaining the situation to all the other people, who had run into the open place right behind me. *Help him!* I yelled. *We have to help him!* Finally, I made them understand what they had to do. Together, with me supervising and the people supplying the muscle, we lifted that tree off my man's leg, and he sat up and then he stood all the way up and then he bent all the way back down again just to pick me up and hold me tight, with his face against my face and lots more salty water coming out of his eyes. It was coming out of all the other people's eyes, too. SO weird.

We helped the man back to the water and into one of the boats and we all paddled back together and then we had a big feast and all the people gave me lots of pats and treats. It was the best, most exciting day ever.

Yours always, Stella

Charles smiled as he stood on the porch of the lodge reading Stella's words. He and Dad and the Bean and Buddy were all packed up and on their way home, but first they had stopped to say good-bye to Frank and Beansie.

Charles loved the way Stella told the story. It really had ended up being the best day ever, even though it had been scary at first to find Beansie trapped under a tree that had fallen the wrong way when he cut it down with his chainsaw. The old man was fine — just a few bruises and no broken bones. Best of all, Charles had a strong feeling that Frank and Beansie had realized what Charles had known all along: that Stella belonged with them forever and ever.

Frank opened the lodge door. She had on a bright smile — so different from the long face she'd worn the day before. Stella lay nestled in her arms.

"We came to say good-bye," said Charles.

"Oh, dear, we'll miss you," she said. "And we can't thank you enough for helping us see the truth — that Stella is part of our family, whether she can hear or not."

"Beansie thinks so, too?" Charles asked.

She nodded. "You have no idea how broken up he was about giving her away. He might have acted he wasn't hurting, but he was. But now he knows he was wrong. This whole sign language thing isn't so hard. I already knew the most important sign of all, didn't I?" She did it again, setting Stella on the floor, then holding up her palms. "Where's Beansie?" she asked the fluffy white pup. "Find Beansie!" The little dog raced into the lodge.

Moments later, Stella came back out — carried in Beansie's arms. She licked the old man's face over and over as Beansie chuckled. "That's my girl," he said, stroking her lovingly. He smiled at Charles. "I hope y'all will come back and see us again next year," he croaked. "We've already signed Emma up to work with us, so we'll have plenty of time to go fishing and hiking with you. I know Stella will be over the moon to see her old friends again."

"We'll be back for sure," Charles promised. "I have to catch that fish that got away. And next time, we'll teach Buddy to ride in a canoe so he doesn't miss all the excitement." Charles knew that Buddy would never forget his fluffy white friend. Neither would Charles. He also knew that Stella had found the best forever home of all: her own.

PUPPY TIPS

Have you ever met a deaf dog? Some dogs are deaf from the time they are born, while other dogs can become deaf as they age. You don't have to feel sorry for a deaf dog; their lives can be as full and happy as any other dogs' lives. If you've ever wondered if your puppy or dog might have trouble hearing, talk to your vet about it. He or she can help you figure out whether there is a problem and give you tips on how to deal with it. Some people like to teach their dogs hand signals even if they are not deaf. These signals can come in handy if the dog ever loses hearing later in life, and they are also just another way to communicate.

Dear Reader,

I enjoyed doing the research to learn more about deaf dogs and how to help them. It was fascinating to watch videos of people communicating with their deaf dogs!

My dog Zipper has excellent hearing. Even so, I have taught him the hand signals for sit, lie down, and come. He doesn't always obey, but he knows what I want him to do.

Yours from the Puppy Place,
Ellen Miles

P.S. For another outdoor puppy adventure, check out Baxter!

ABOUT THE AUTHOR

Ellen Miles loves dogs, which is why she has a great time writing the Puppy Place books. And guess what? She loves cats, too! (In fact, her very first pet was a beautiful tortoiseshell cat named Jenny.) That's why she came up with the Kitty Corner series. Ellen lives in Vermont and loves to be outdoors every day, walking, biking, skiing, or swimming, depending on the season. She also loves to read, cook, explore her beautiful state, play with dogs, and hang out with friends and family.

Visit Ellen at www.ellenmiles.net.